The HUGE BAG of WORRIES

The
HUGE BAG
of WORRIES

Illustrations by
Frank Rodgers

By Virginia Ironside

Hodder
Children's
Books

For Finn and Will Russell-Cobb

HODDER CHILDREN'S BOOKS

First published in Great Britain in 1996 by Macdonald Young Books
This edition published in 2016 by Hodder and Stoughton

14

Text copyright © Virginia Ironside, 1996
Illustrations copyright © Frank Rodgers, 1996

A CIP catalogue record for this book is available from the British Library.

ISBN 978 0 340 90317 9

Printed in China

The paper and board used in this book are from wood from responsible sources.

Hodder Children's Books
An imprint of
Hachette Children's Group
Part of Hodder and Stoughton
Carmelite House
50 Victoria Embankment
London EC4Y 0DZ

An Hachette UK Company
www.hachette.co.uk

www.hachettechildrens.co.uk

Jenny had always been happy. She had a lovely mum and dad, a great brother (well, most of the time…), she had a best friend at school and she liked her teacher. And then, of course, there was Loftus.

But recently she had been getting gloomier and gloomier.
It wasn't just one thing; it was everything.

She worried that she
was getting too fat,

that Loftus had fleas

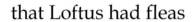

and that her best friend
was going away.

She worried that she was getting bad marks at school and she thought she heard someone whispering about her in the playground…

she worried when her mum and dad had an argument…

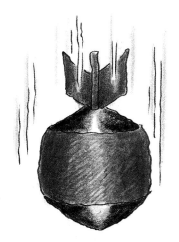

she even worried about wars and bombs…

until one day she woke to find…

...a HUGE BAG OF WORRIES.

The bag followed her everywhere…

to school,

to swimming,

to the toilet,

and it stuck by her even when she was watching TV.

She tried ignoring it…
but it didn't work.

She tried throwing it away…   but it always came back.

She tried to lock it out,

but when she got back to her bedroom, there it was, waiting for her.

It was like a horrible shadow she couldn't get rid of.

What could she do?

She asked her brother for help. But he was busy with his
computer game, and all he said was: "I don't know what
you are talking about. *I* don't have any worries."

After that she didn't feel like asking anyone else. She knew
she'd only feel stupid.

Mum would probably say: "You've got no worries that I can see. You're a lucky girl. You've got your health, your friends, your family – what more do you want?" So she decided not to tell her.

Dad might know what to do.
But then she thought again.
No. Dad had enough
worries of his own.
She couldn't ask him.

Every day things got worse.

The bag got bigger...   and bigger...

and bigger.

She couldn't sleep because it kept tossing and turning beside her all night.

To make matters worse, the bag dragged around her feet so much when she was walking to school that she was late and the teacher was cross.

Jenny couldn't tell her what had happened, and anyway she knew what she would say: "You've got too many worries! In future, leave that bag at home!"

When Jenny told her best friend about the bag, she suggested that Jenny locked it up in a cupboard and tried not to think about it. "That's what I do," she said.

But it just didn't work.

Even Loftus couldn't help.

He tried his best and
barked like mad,

but the bag stood its ground.

One morning Jenny woke up, got dressed and walked down the road. She'd had enough. The tears started rolling down her cheeks. She sat on a garden wall and put her head in her hands. She thought she'd have to live with the bag forever.

Then she heard a voice and, looking up, she saw the kindly face of the old lady who lived next door.

"Goodness!" said the old lady. "What on earth is that HUGE bag of worries?"

Through her tears, Jenny explained how it had followed her for weeks, and got bigger and bigger, and just wouldn't go away.

"Now let's just open it up and see what's inside," said the old lady.

But Jenny said she couldn't. If she opened the bag, the worries might jump out and who knew what might happen then.

"Nonsense," said the old lady firmly. "There's nothing a worry hates more than being seen. If you have any worries, however small, the secret is to let them out slowly, one by one, and show them to someone else. They'll soon go away."

So Jenny opened the bag.

The old lady sorted the worries into groups.

Jenny was astonished to see how small they looked when
they were out in the open.

Half the worries disappeared because lots of worries just hate the light of day.

As for the rest, the old lady put some in her shopping basket to deal with herself;

some she sent packing because she said they belonged to other people;

some she just blew a kiss to;

and some she said were worries that everyone had,
even Jenny's family, her friends and her teacher.

And as for the bag…

Other great Hodder picture books perfect to share with children:

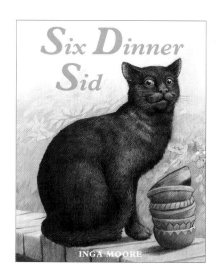

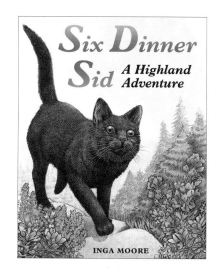

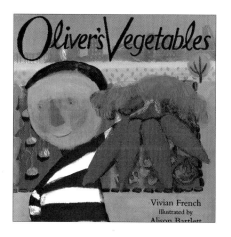